DANCING IN THE MOONLIGHT

ROSE MARIE MEUWISSEN

DANCING IN THE MOONLIGHT

BY

ROSE MARIE MEUWISSEN

Dancing in the Moonlight
by
Rose Marie Meuwissen

Dancing in the Moonlight
Digital/Print Edition
Copyright 2013 by Rose Marie Meuwissen
https://www.rosemariemeuwissen.com

Published in the United States of America
Nordic Publishing
Edited by Laura Breck
Cover Design by Rose Marie Meuwissen

❀ Created with Vellum

To Monty and Rose's cabin 'up North' on Mille Lacs Lake where I spent many weekends over the years with my children enjoying fishing for walleyes, riding jet skis, making s'mores by the fire and gazing at the star filled sky in the evening.

A MINNESOTA LAKES ROMANCE

MILLE LACS LAKE

*Anna Thorstad never imagined reopening her parents' lake
cabin would also open her heart to love again.*

A MINNESOTA LAKES ROMANCE

MINNESOTA

Land of 10,000 Lakes

DANCING IN THE MOONLIGHT

By

Rose Marie Meuwissen

CHAPTER 1

Anna Thorstad rubbed her eyes as the setting sun began to drop below the tree filled horizon. The drive up to Mille Lacs Lake from the Twin Cities generally takes about three very long hours. Today, there was a lot of traffic. Way more, than she remembered, but then it had been a long time since she made the drive up North, as they say, for the weekend. It amazed her how a person's whole frame of mind changed once you reached the miles and miles of tall wild grasses and forests of pine trees. The drive brought on a feeling of serenity you just couldn't find in the Twin Cities. A totally relaxing feeling, making one believe all your worries and stress could be left behind. The lengthy flight from Phoenix involved spending far too much time sitting around in airports and then of course the waiting in line to get a rental car. She knew she still had almost an hour until she would finally arrive at the cabin.

Her parents, considered snowbirds, spent the summers up in Minnesota at the cabin and the winters down in Phoenix, but this last year their health deteriorated which forced them to spend the summer in Phoenix. Summers in

Phoenix tend to be brutally hot which probably didn't help their health issues. Needless to say, their deaths earlier in the year were unanticipated. Ultimately, she had no idea what condition the cabin would be in when she got there, since it had been shut down for almost two years now.

Her head lights shown like bright beacons down the gravel road. Then she saw it, a deer standing in the middle of the road and her foot hit the brake immediately. As soon as her car began sliding down the road on the gravel surface, the deer quickly dashed off into the ditch on its merry way. Anna stopped the car just as it ran off.

Her hands trembled as she rested her head on the steering wheel. She never dreamed she would be making this drive by herself either. Dan, her ex-husband, should be here with her, supporting her in her hour of need, but no here she was an unemployed, forty-five year old divorced woman on her own and all alone. That was fine. She didn't need the two timing son of a bitch! She could do this all by herself. However, she really didn't need a deer smashed into the windshield of her rental car right now. At this moment, she was completely unsure why she had decided against booking a hotel room in Bloomington near the airport and instead chose to drive up to the cabin alone at night. She took her foot off the brake and continued driving down the dark road, alone.

In the dark it was hard to find identifying landmarks to show if she already passed the entrance to the cabin that lay hidden behind all those glorious old trees loaded down with thousands of green leaves. Finally, she saw it. The Viking Ship mail box. It had been her Christmas present to her parents five years ago. She ordered the Viking Ship mailbox so it would be easier for them to find the entrance road leading to the cabin. The irony of that fact was unbelievably eerie since she certainly would've driven past the cabin entrance road if it hadn't been there. She drove down the winding driveway and stopped in front of the attached garage. Unfortunately the garage door opener would not work because the electricity was turned off. She left the car lights on so she could see the front door of the cabin. As she dug the keys out of her purse, she looked up just in time to see two raccoons run past the front of the car through her headlights.

"God, I hope they left and aren't coming back," Anna said as she watched them scurry into the wooded area behind the cabin.

After Anna assured herself the raccoons left the driveway area, she cautiously opened the door, got out of the car and quickly walked up to the familiar side entrance door painted black and adorned with red and teal rosemaling. The key slipped easily into the lock and the door opened as she turned the door knob and slowly walked inside. She reached out her hand and it touched something solid. *Thank heavens the flashlight sat on the bench by the door.* She picked it up, pressing the on button, praying it still worked. A beam of light pointed directly in front of her and she immediately walked down the steps to the basement where the electrical box was located. She opened the door and flipped the power switch on. Immediately the light came on over her head. *Thanks Dad!* Her dad always left that particular light on so he would know if the power came on. She let out a sigh of relief and walked back up the steps to see a man standing outside the screen door. Anna couldn't help it, she screamed.

CHAPTER 2

"Anna, is it you?" Gabe asked.

"Who are you?" Anna asked, not answering him.

"Gabe Setterstrom."

Anna tried to calm herself so she could focus on what he'd just said. He said his name like she should recognize it and him. Gabe Setterstrom. *Who was he?*

"Yes, I'm Anna. How do you know who I am?"

"My parent's cabin is next door. I saw a car drive up. Just wanted to see who was over here since I always keep an eye on the cabin for your parents."

Anna took in every inch of the man standing in front of her on the other side of the screen door. Definitely attractive. Broad shoulders, tan chiseled face, with sun bleached blond hair and an amazingly sexy smile. *He was hot but who the hell was he?* She didn't have a clue.

"Forgive me, but it's been a long day. You live next door?" Anna turned off her flashlight.

Gabe laughed. "I guess you don't remember me. It's been a long time. I'd say about twenty plus years. You probably remember me more as a skinny young guy named Gabriel who was madly in love with you."

"That's you? I would never have guessed."

"Now you remember me? "

"You look totally different than I remember." Anna continued to stare at Gabe.

"I hope that's good." Gabe grinned.

"Definitely."

"If you want, I can help you get everything turned back on and make sure you have everything under control." Gabe stuck one hand in his jean pocket while he waited for her reply.

"I'd like that."

Gabe walked in and began checking the whole cabin to make sure all the important things worked, like the lights, appliances, etc. Anna followed him and watched him go through the exact same routine her dad used to do. But her dad was gone. The loss of her parents still cut deeply. Her heart ached. She walked into the kitchen and sat down at the table. She couldn't stop the tears, as they slowly ran down her cheeks.

Gabe walked over and sat down on the chair next to hers. "You okay?"

"No."

"Want to talk about it?" he asked and gently touched her hand.

"I don't think I've ever been up here when they weren't here. Watching you check everything reminded me of my dad doing the exact same thing when we arrived. It made me realize I would never see him do it again." Anna gave way to the pain caused by losing her parents and cried. Even after the funeral she hadn't suffered pain like she felt at this very moment. The cabin contained years and years of their history together as a family, a place where many of her best memories were made. Ones she would always remember.

Gabe put his arm around her shoulder and pulled her into his arms. "It's okay. Under these circumstances crying is probably good. I still miss my parents and they died five years ago."

Anna pulled back slightly and looked up at Gabe. His bright blue eyes now glistened with moisture and she remembered the boy she used to talk to for hours under the moonlight while sitting on the dock. "I'm sorry. I didn't know." The sad truth was she hadn't even thought about him once after she'd left Minnesota for college, much less his parents. In fact, she'd only been back up to the cabin a handful of times since then and he hadn't been up there on those occasions.

"It gets better as time goes on. You'll never forget them, but the pain eases up." Gabe reached over to brush long strands of blonde hair away from her face while staring into her glazed green eyes. He kissed her full pouting lips.

Anna kissed him back. Her emotions ran high and the kiss brought her desire to the surface. "Gabe, I need the pain to go away. At least right now for a little while." She kissed him wildly, unbuttoning his shirt, running her roving fingers over his broad chest. She moved closer and straddled him sitting on his lap, pressing her body into his.

He kissed her back, pushing her extremely revealing, low cut tank top down a little more so he could cup her bare breast in his hand. Then abruptly he stopped and pulled back slightly.

"Anna, we can't."

"Please. Losing them hurts so much and kissing you feels so good," Anna pleaded.

"I won't deny that. God, Anna, I'm a grown man. I'd like nothing better than to carry you into one of these bedrooms and have wild crazy sex with you. But that's all it would be tonight. You wouldn't even be able to look me straight in the eyes in the morning."

Anna pulled back and stood up. He was right. Totally right. She wanted to have sex with Gabe for all the wrong reasons. Mainly she just wanted to experience pure pleasure tonight instead of the overwhelming pain embedded deep inside from the loss of her parents.

"I'm going to go over to my parent's cabin—my cabin—take a cold shower and try to go to sleep. Will you be all right?"

"Yes. I'm sorry. Oh my God! Are you married?" Anna's hand went to her heart as she waited for his answer.

"No. And you don't have any reason to be sorry." Gabe gave her a reassuring smile.

"It's just being in this cabin set off so many crazy emotions inside me."

"I get it. How about breakfast in the morning and we can talk about it? Besides my frig has food in it and yours is empty," Gabe stated while showing off his sexy smile.

"Deal. What time are you serving breakfast?"

"Let's say nine," Gabe said and walked toward the door. Anna followed. He turned around toward her, took her in his arms and kissed her with a passionate deep soul searching kiss that left them both breathless. He smiled. "Always leave them wanting more."

"What?"

"Just wanted to make sure you show up for breakfast in the morning." Gabe grinned and walked out the door.

CHAPTER 3

Anna stood at the door watching his retreating back as he walked up the path to his cabin next door. What did he mean when he said he was madly in love with her back some twenty years ago? Maybe she really blew it back then and didn't even know it? She definitely needed to check into the situation tomorrow when she talked to him during breakfast. She opened the door and walked out to the car to get her bags. She didn't bother to put the car in the garage. It was late and she was tired, the car would be fine sitting in the driveway for the night. She walked back in the house and locked the door behind her.

Now to decide which bedroom to sleep in. The master bedroom would always be her parents' room so she walked into her bedroom. It looked exactly the same as when she was young. Mom kept it the same for her. The tears rolled down her cheeks. Over the years she only came back a couple of times. Busy raising children, working and doing too many other more important things prevented her from even coming back to take a summer vacation in Minnesota. But no matter how long her parents lived in Phoenix, they still called Minnesota home. This cabin was where they became a family and where all the best memories came from, at least the ones she remembered.

Anna got ready for bed and walked through the house just to be sure everything was okay. Unfortunately, every room she walked into reminded her of her parents. She needed to sleep, she was tired and it was after midnight. She glanced out the patio screen door at the moonlight shining on the calm waters of the lake. Thousands and thousands of stars only seen up in northern Minnesota sprinkled over an otherwise clear sky. She left the patio door and curtain open, and then crawled into bed. As she closed her eyes she could have sworn she saw her mother and father standing in the doorway saying, "Good Night." *Must really be tired*. Minutes later she was sound asleep.

Anna awoke to morning sunbeams warming her cheek. Her eyes opened to a beautiful morning sunrise with a clear blue sky and gentle waves lapping on the shore. She rolled over and picked up her phone to check the time. Eight o'clock. Time to get up, she had a breakfast date!

She picked out a pair of jean capris, a black tank top, and a light jacket since the morning temperatures usually remained cool. An hour later, Anna checked her reflection in the mirror one last time before leaving. Not bad, she thought. She walked out, closed the door behind her and walked over to Gabe's cabin. His door stood open and as a result she could see through the screen to the kitchen. Gabe looked over and smiled at her.

"Come on in. Perfect timing. Just finished. Have a seat." Gabe motioned toward the table.

Anna walked in and sat down at the kitchen table. She

scanned the room. Everything appeared clean and neat. Gabe dished up their breakfast consisting of bacon, eggs, and pancakes. He set their plates on the table and sat down across from her.

"It looks delicious. Thanks." Anna took a bite of the bacon, as her stomach growled reminding her that last night she didn't take time to eat anything for supper.

"How'd you sleep?" Gabe asked.

"Okay. Extremely weird though. I haven't slept there in a long time and never alone."

"You'll get used to it."

"Tell me about yourself." Anna took a sip of orange juice. "Where you live, work, any kids?"

"I married the first girl I fell in love with after you. Unfortunately, don't think she ever really fell in love with me. We managed to stay married for fifteen years before she left. Said she didn't love me, never had, and wanted to fall in love with someone, consequently she needed a divorce. Happened six years ago, right before my parents died in a car accident." Gabe got up and poured himself another glass of orange juice. "I'm a commercial airline pilot. Since I'm gone a lot, I keep a condo in Apple Valley and live up here when I'm off. My one and only daughter is fifteen and lives with her mother. Whenever she can, she comes up here to spend a few days with me."

"I'm sorry about the divorce. That things didn't work out. Mine didn't either. He divorced me for his young sales associate about two years ago. My son and daughter are both in college. One in Seattle and one in San Diego. "

"Do you live in the Twin Cities?" Gabe asked.

"No. Phoenix."

"That's why you haven't been around," Gabe said. "What brings you back up here?"

"I came to pack up the cabin and put it on the market."

Anna looked hesitant. "But after seeing it and being flooded with wonderful memories of my childhood, I'm not sure that's the right thing to do."

"I experienced the same feelings after my parents died. I wanted to pack it up and sell, too." Gabe stated. "But after spending just one weekend up here, I knew I couldn't sell it. Hell, I didn't need the money and it proved to be a great place to just get away from the craziness of life in the cities and just relax."

"I know. All the stress faded away once I got up here. Being on the lake is a whole different world. Very peaceful."

Anna watched Gabe pick up their empty plates, walk over to the sink and begin rinsing them off. "Say, when's the last time you actually went out on the lake?" he asked.

"It's been years. A very long time. I'm not sure if the boat even runs."

"Mine does. Would you like to go out on the lake this afternoon? We can even do some fishing if you want. Unless, of course, you have other plans."

"No plans. In fact I don't have a clue what I'm doing. A boat ride and fishing sounds great. I'd love to."

"I'll pack us a lunch since you don't have any food," he laughed. "Meet me down at the dock at one."

"Thanks for the delicious breakfast. See you at the dock." Anna left a smiling Gabe at the screen door. She couldn't help smiling back. And smiling was something she hadn't been doing much of lately.

CHAPTER 4

Anna met Gabe at the dock promptly at one. He, of course, was already down there getting the boat ready. He smiled when he saw her approaching.

"Ready to catch some walleye?" he asked.

"Yes, but I just realized I don't have a fishing license."

"I picked one up at the bait store this morning. You're good. Remember how to catch walleye?"

Anna laughed. "I remember you teaching me when we were very young."

"Then we're in good shape. We can have walleye for dinner."

Anna got in and took a seat while Gabe lowered the lift until the boat floated in the water. The motor started and they skimmed across the water as Anna's memories of being on the lake in a boat with Gabe many years ago floated through her mind.

It was a warm day but the fish were biting and they soon caught their limit. Anna wore her bikini and stretched out on the back of the boat to soak up some sun. She lifted her cover-up dress and slid it over her head while watching for

Gabe's reaction. She assumed he liked what he saw since he smiled as he took off his shirt. An obvious and strong chemistry existed between them. Anna hadn't slept with or felt attracted to anyone since the divorce. She knew Gabe was right about last night though. But now it was a new day and she still wanted to have hot crazy sex with him.

"Want some sunscreen?" he asked.

Perfect, she thought. She never burned, but he didn't have to know that. "Oh, yes. Can you put some on my back?" And without waiting for his reply, she rolled over on her stomach. Seconds later the lotion dripped onto her back and strong male hands gently massaged it into her smooth skin. Oh yes, she thought, she wanted to feel those hands all over her body. Wanted to be touched again. Wanted to press her body against his rock solid chest. Basically, she just wanted to feel alive again. And right now she felt the most alive she had in a long time. Gabe had awakened her sleeping body, tantalizing it with the prospect of being brought back to life sexually. It had been way too long. And of course she wouldn't mind falling in love again, either.

Gabe finished caressing Anna's body with lotion and took in the sight of her almost bare back and sexy butt in the tiny bikini bottom. His mind remained totally fixated on sex. He needed to keep control of his sexual desires because he didn't want to scare her away. He greatly enjoyed the sight laid out in front of him, but then she sat up and their eyes met, each knowing what the other was thinking.

Anna held out her hand. "Here, let me put some on your back so you don't get burned."

Gabe handed her the bottle, turned his back toward her, happy to oblige because then she wouldn't see what her almost naked body did to his body, one part in particular. Because he was undeniably hard. Her hands touched his back, sliding gently over his shoulders, spreading the lotion.

He feared he would lose it. He gritted his teeth and enjoyed every pleasurable moment. When he couldn't take it anymore, he turned around and took her in his arms and kissed her. She kissed him back and tongue met tongue in a sensual tango. He wanted to take her right there, but he knew they couldn't do it in the boat. Not for their first time. He pulled back and looked into her searching eyes.

"Not here," he stated huskily. "But we are finishing this later."

"Deal," Anna confirmed. "I'm counting on it." She smiled and lay back down on her towel.

Gabe laughed. "Definitely my kind of woman." Little did she know how long he had waited for her. Just one problem, he knew he would not be able to let her get away this time. This time he would do whatever it took to win her heart.

CHAPTER 5

A few hours later, they pulled up to the dock and Gabe secured the boat back into the boat lift. Anna helped carry the cooler and towels up to the cabin.

"I'll get these fish cleaned for supper. I'm sure you have things you need to sort through in your parent's cabin. Dinner will be served at six." Gabe brushed her lips with a quick kiss.

"That another one of those, 'Leave them wanting more,' tactics?" Anna laughed.

"You bet. Did it work?" Gabe asked over his shoulder as he headed to his garage to clean the fish.

"I'll be counting the minutes." Anna laughed and walked to her parent's cabin.

Once inside she walked out onto the fully screened porch overlooking the lake. An absolutely beautiful view and definitely not one you could see in Phoenix. She pulled her phone out of her pocket and called the realtor she was supposed to meet with in the morning to discuss selling the cabin.

"Hi, this is Anna. We have an appointment tomorrow morning."

"Yes, how are you doing? I'm looking forward to meeting you," the realtor answered.

"I'm sorry but I'm going to have to cancel. I'm going to need some more time to decide if selling the cabin is the right option for me at this time." Anna walked over to the side window where she could see Gabe cleaning the fish.

"The market is picking up and we should be able to get you a good price at this time."

"I will call you if I decide to sell," Anna said while staring at Gabe's tan muscular chest as he made short work of filleting the walleye. She didn't even wait for the realtor's response. "Goodbye." Anna disconnected the call and walked back inside the cabin.

Promptly at six, Anna walked over to Gabe's cabin. On her way, she could smell the fish frying on the stove. It smelled just like she remembered when her dad would fry the fish they'd caught. She knocked lightly on the screen door and walked in.

"It smells good! Can I hire you to be my cook?" Anna laughed.

"What would you give me in return?" Gabe asked as he set the platter of fish on the table along with a bowl of fried potatoes, onions and green peppers.

"I'm sure something could be arranged," Anna smiled.

This time after dinner, Anna cleared the table and loaded the dishwasher. The sun was setting as they headed down to the beach afterwards.

"I had a great day, Gabe. Thank you," Anna said as they walked down the hill to the beach.

"No problem. I definitely enjoyed your company."

"I haven't eaten walleye for a long time. And definitely not *fresh* walleye. This is delicious. You are a great cook!"

"Good thing since I like to eat good food and I have to cook for myself."

Gabe lit the fire and soon they had a blazing bonfire. He'd brought down marshmallows, chocolate bars, graham crackers and long handled sticks to make s'mores.

Anna put the marshmallows on the sticks as they listened to some old '80s tunes playing from the speakers on the hill. She placed one toasted marshmallow on each graham cracker with three chocolate squares, and then placed another graham cracker on top, gently pressing down on the hot marshmallow to melt the chocolate onto the graham crackers, ultimately making a hot sticky gooey mess that catered to every chocolate craving you possessed. She handed one to Gabe and then took a bite of the other.

They sat in their chairs with their stomachs completely sated, watching the fire blaze against the backdrop of calm waves lapping the shore, and a full moon lighting the sky and horizon. Song after song from their younger years wafted out of the speakers as they sang along.

'Dancing in the Moonlight' played and Gabe stood extending his hand out to Anna. "Can I have this dance?"

Anna didn't answer but instead stood, took his hand and followed Gabe down to the firmer sand closer to the shore. He took her in his arms and they began swaying to the music while they sang along to the words of the song. When the song ended, Gabe kissed her. Like the fire blazing behind them, their bodies radiated an intense fire, each craving the other, pressing their bodies together, igniting passions held at bay far too long.

"I have to put the fire out." Gabe broke the embrace, walked over to pick up a shovel and began shoveling sand on the fire.

Anna watched silently as the fire died before her eyes. But the fire inside her still raged wildly as Gabe walked back to her and took her hand.

"My place or yours?" he asked as he led her up the hill to the cabins.

"Yours."

CHAPTER 6

Gabe opened the door to his cabin and pulled Anna inside immediately pulling her up against his hard chest and possessively devouring her lips and mouth. Almost frantically they removed their jackets and dropped them to the floor.

Anna didn't hold back, she kissed him with every fiber of her being. Her breathing grew rapid as she clung to him while he carried her into the bedroom, laying her on the bed. She slid off her shoes and pulled her tank top over her head. Gabe pulled his t-shirt over his head while sliding off his sandals. Moments later he hovered over her, filling his memory with pictures of his beautiful Anna and then his lips found hers, first a slow sensual kiss, then quickening the tempo which led to a frenzied devouring kiss. He left a trail of kisses down her neck to her breasts, sliding her bra straps down and quickly discarding it as his mouth found her taut breasts. Gabe stood up and dropped his jeans and boxers to the floor while Anna slid her jeans and thong to the floor.

He watched the fire blaze in Anna's eyes as he caressed her body. His hand slid down between her legs to her wet entrance. Her body arched and he knew without asking she was ready. Anna nodded. Gabe quickly slid a condom on and entered her slowly, picking up speed rapidly as their bodies writhed together. He waited until he heard her moans of pleasure, then he let go of his control and allowed his body to reach a mind-blowing orgasm. Gabe rolled over to lie next to her, turning her mouth toward him for a kiss.

"Wow." Anna smiled. "I never knew it could be like that."

Gabe had no idea what her ex-husband considered good sex, but obviously it hadn't been good for Anna. He'd experienced bad sex and good sex. And he'd experienced okay sex —mainly with his ex. Hands down though, with Anna definitely the best sex ever. Admitting it, an entirely different thing though. "It was even better than I anticipated all these years." *So much for not admitting it!*

"What do you mean?"

"Maybe it's just a guy thing, but we have a tendency to think the one that got away would've been the best. And this was." There he'd said it. Probably shouldn't have, but he did.

Anna rolled over on top of him and kissed him. They never made it out of bed until the next morning, after many more hours of fabulous sex.

Anna woke up to an empty bed. She could smell bacon cooking. She got up, took a shower, dressed and went down the hall to the kitchen, totally unsure how to act after last night. As soon as Gabe heard her enter the room he looked up and smiled a reassuring smile, immediately relaxing her.

"Good morning, Anna."

"Good morning. It smells delicious whatever you're cooking. Possibly bacon?"

Gabe walked over and took her in his arms and kissed her.

"This is awkward," Anna said.

"Only if we let it be," Gabe stated. "We should probably talk about where we want this to go."

"I know. I live in Phoenix. I don't know but I've always heard long distance relationships don't work well."

"I'm a pilot. I can fly anywhere in a matter of hours. Have you ever thought about moving back to Minnesota?"

"Honestly, no. Never had a reason to." Anna knew she had no reason to stay in Phoenix. Heck she didn't even have a job. Thankfully she received a nice settlement in the divorce and didn't need to.

"Anna, you never said where you worked," Gabe stated.

"I don't. Not anymore. Formerly the Office Manager for my ex-husband's car dealership. Actually, it was our dealership. He wanted to buy me out in the divorce. In the end, I took the buyout because I just couldn't work with the both of them anymore. So right now, I'm unemployed, but I don't really need to work." *Had she said too much?*

"I don't want this to be just a weekend of great sex with the love of my life." Gabe smiled. "I'd like to see where this could go."

"It just seems immensely complicated."

They ate and Anna walked back to her parents' cabin to pack so she could make her evening flight back to Phoenix. She turned everything off and closed up the cabin. Gabe met her in the driveway.

"Anna, here is my business card with my cell phone and email. Call me. I really want to spend some time with you and see where this goes. We're both adults. We've been around the block. I like what I see. We have history, even though it was a long time ago. Maybe this is our second chance." Gabe handed her the card and kissed her with a long deep kiss.

Anna got in her rental car.

"I've never been one to jump into things. I always have to think things through. Give me some time to work it out in my mind."

"I'll be up here for two weeks. Been flying long enough I can arrange my schedule to work two weeks and have the next two weeks off. Call me anytime," he said. "And just to let you know, great sex like what we just had is hard to find."

CHAPTER 7

Anna started the car and drove down the driveway watching Gabe in her rear view mirror until she could no longer see him. She turned onto the main road and headed to the Twin Cities. As she drove, she kept thinking about Gabe. It must've been meant to be, them being up there at the same time. She'd made the decision not to sell the cabin and it wasn't just because Gabe was next door. No, it was because she could sense her parents' presence in every room of the cabin. It was filled with memories she wanted to keep forever. She wanted the cabin to make new memories with her children and future grandchildren, too. And if she could start a new life with Gabe, all the better. It was the best sex she'd ever had, but besides that it was the best weekend she'd had in a long, long time. She pulled the car over in the town of Isle, an hour later and pulled into a parking lot.

What was she doing? She didn't have any reason to go back to Phoenix. All she had was an empty house. Her ex-husband had the company and his girlfriend, her children were off at college, and her parents were gone forever. She finally found someone who made her feel alive again and what had she done? She'd left. She needed to start thinking about what was best for her, instead of everyone else.

Anna turned the car around and drove back to the cabin. She pulled up in the driveway to what was now her cabin.

She saw Gabe open his door and walk outside. He walked up to her car. "Did you forget something?"

Anna opened the car door and got out. She put her arms around his neck and smiled up at him. "Yes, you." She kissed him.

Gabe smiled. "Does that mean you're all mine for the next two weeks?"

"Realized there really wasn't any reason I needed to be back in Phoenix, since I don't have a job to go to anymore. So let's see what happens."

"More great sex. That's one of the things that will happen."

Anna took Gabe's hand and they walked over to Gabe's parents' cabin, now his cabin, next to her parents' cabin, now her cabin. Anna smiled hoping this was the beginning of a new life with Gabe, who she knew could easily become the love of her life. She smiled. For the first time in a very long time, she was confident she had made the right decision.

Gabe opened the screen door and they walked hand in hand into his cabin, a place where she experienced security and love again after feeling lost and alone for too long. She wasn't about to let Gabe slip through her fingers this time! She was right where she wanted to be.

The End

RECIPE

Pan Fried Fresh Walleye

2-4 Fresh Walleye Filets
  1 Cup Flour
  2 Tbsp Old Bay Seasoning Mix (Or similar seasoning mix)
  1 Tsp Ground Black Pepper
  ½ Cup Canola Oil (Add more if needed)

Filet fish, being sure to remove all the bones. Rinse and pat dry.

Mix flour and seasoning together in a pie tin.

Pre-heat a large stainless steel fry pan over medium heat.

Pour enough oil into pan to cover bottom with a ½ inch depth.

Dip filet in flour mixture, turning to be sure it is completely covered.

Place filets in hot oil, leaving space in between each one.

Fry until golden brown. When done the edges will easily come free of the bottom of the pan with tongs and can be turned over. Let cook a few more minutes before removing.

Place on a cooling rack lined with paper towels to prevent them from becoming soggy.

May be placed in warm oven to keep warm.

ABOUT THE AUTHOR

ROSE MARIE MEUWISSEN

Rose Marie Meuwissen, a first-generation Norwegian American born and raised in Minnesota, always tries to incorporate her Norwegian heritage into her writing. After receiving a BA in Marketing from Concordia University, a Masters in Creative Writing from Hamline University soon followed. Minnesota is still where she calls home.

She has traveled around the world, including Scandinavia, but still has many places to see, enjoys attending Scandinavian events, writing conferences and is usually busy writing Minnesota Lakes Contemporary Romances, Viking Time Travel Romances or Norwegian Traditions Children's Books.

Visit her at www.rosemariemeuwissen.com or www.realnorwegianseatlutefisk.com.

NOVELS:

Taking Chances—a contemporary romance novel set in Minnesota and Arizona.

Married by Saturday—a contemporary romance novel set in Minnesota and Montana.

Looking for Mr. Right—a contemporary internet dating romance novel set on Prior Lake in Minnesota—***Coming soon!***

NOVELLAS:

·

Annika—A Christmas Romance—a contemporary romance set in Minnesota with a Nordic theme during the Christmas Holidays.

Skol! Viking Blonde Ale—a contemporary romance set in Minnesota at an Autumn festival complete with a fortune teller, ale and Vikings!

Choosing to Live—a Norwegian woman's journey during WWII to survive the Nazi Occupation of Norway—*Coming soon!*

MINNESOTA LAKES ROMANCE NOVELETTES:

A Kiss Under the Northern Lights—a Summer romance set in Ely, Minnesota on Big Lake.

Dancing in the Moonlight—a Summer romance set in Malmo, Minnesota on Mille Lacs Lake.

Hot Summer Nights—a Summer romance set in Prior Lake, Minnesota on Prior Lake.

Railroad Ties—an Autumn romance set in Two Harbors, Minnesota on Lake Superior.

Blizzard of Love—a Winter romance set in Lutsen, Minnesota on Lake Superior.

Nor-Way to Love—a Spring romance set in Minneapolis, Minnesota on Lake Harriet.

Old Yule Log Fires—a Christmas romance set in Excelsior, Minnesota on Lake Minnetonka.

A Date for Valentine's Day—a Valentine romance set in Minnetonka Beach, Minnesota at the Lafayette Country Club on Lake Minnetonka.

Dance of Love—a Fall Festival romance set at the Renaissance Fair in Shakopee, Minnesota.

CHILDREN'S BOOKS—REAL NORWEGIAN'S SERIES:

Real Norwegians Eat Lutefisk—a Children's book about the tradition of Lutefisk presented in both English and Norwegian.

Real Norwegians Eat Rømmegrøt—the second Children's book in the series about the tradition of Rømmegrøt presented in both English and Norwegian.

Real Norwegians Eat Lefse—the third Children's book in the series about the tradition of Lefse presented in both English and Norwegian.

Real Norwegians Eat Krumkake—the fourth Children's book in the series about the tradition of Krumkake presented in both English and Norwegian—*Coming next!*

MICRO-MINI NOVELETTE—COMING SOON!

Christmas Notes—a collection of Christmas prose poems to warm the heart during the Christmas season.

PREVIEW

Continue Reading for a Preview of:

Married by Saturday

By
Rose Marie Meuwissen

PREVIEW COPYRIGHT INFO

Published by
Satin Romance
An Imprint of Melange Books, LLC
White Bear Lake, MN 55110
www.satinromance.com

Married by Saturday ~ Copyright 2016 by Rose Marie
Meuwissen
ISBN: 978-1-68046-420-7

MARRIED BY SATURDAY

A MINNESOTA LAKES ROMANCE

Brittany's life was spiraling out of control and she still needed a groom by Saturday or her father would lose everything he'd spent his life working for. The stranger she just met may be the hero she's been looking for her whole life. Regardless, he would suffice as a groom for the wedding ceremony.

Taylor wasn't even looking for a woman and definitely not a bride, when he received an unorthodox marriage proposal from a beautiful trucker.

Can they find true love after the wedding to make their dreams of a happily ever after a reality?

CHAPTER 1

Married by Saturday. She could pull it off. But only if she could find a groom. It really shouldn't be all that difficult. She was a determined woman. She would do it, even if she had to marry a perfect stranger.

Miles and miles of flat, deserted highway merged into the setting sun of Montana. Brittany's shiny gold eighteen-wheeler, loaded with chrome, glistened in the sun's rays as it rolled down the concrete road alone.

Alone was just where Brittany wanted to be right now. On a spur of the moment decision, the huge truck rolled to a halt at the scenic rest area. The majestic mountains of Yellowstone loomed on the horizon, and the cool air was fresh and clean, a far cry from city air.

Brittany was not a typical truck driver. She drove only on rare occasions, when she needed to get away—away from Minneapolis and the rat race. Her favorite runs were to the new truck plant in Newark, California, to pick up a new truck, or to Salt Lake City, Utah, to pick up a new trailer. She was on her way to the latter after a minor detour to Red Lodge.

Dressed in a fitted ivory western style shirt, skintight jeans, tan cowboy boots, and a matching ivory cowboy hat, Brittany felt at ease as she stepped down out of the truck. She was average in height, about 5'4", with a slim and trim body to equal any fashion model's shape. Her tan face resembled the face of an Old Norse goddess, the forehead, and cheekbones high, and proud full lips, with skin a golden tan from many days spent in the sun, and sparkling, golden amber-brown eyes.

Staring at the setting sun, a warm, light wind blew gently through her silky, long, golden blonde hair, and her eyes reflected the sun as if they were pools of firelight. She portrayed a picturesque impression of beauty and peace, even though her thoughts were in turmoil. Just then, another lonely truck rolled down the highway giving Brittany an appreciative toot of his horn. Coming back to the present from her deep thoughts, she smiled and tipped her hat in recognition as she headed back to her truck, the Golden Girl. Time to get moving if she wanted to make the Red Lodge Café before dark.

Back on the road again, Brittany focused on her problem. It was time to find a solution. The problem was marriage, and the deadline was less than a week from today. The pressure from her father's unspoken words proved too much for her, so she left Minneapolis bright and early for the mountains of Montana that promised quiet and solitude.

Making decisions was not usually a problem. She knew how to solve problems. The process was simple—define the problem, list the alternatives, and go with the best solution. But there just wasn't a feasible solution to this problem. This was the twenty-first century, and people just shouldn't have to get married unless they wanted to. But leave it to her grandfather to put her in this position. He'd been old when he wrote the will, and he must've thought he was helping her somehow. But how, was beyond her. The worst part was she needed to be married by her twenty-fifth birthday, which was next Saturday, or wait five more years to receive her two-million-dollar inheritance.

Brittany believed in marriage and wanted to marry some-day, but the right person just hadn't come along. Most of the men she met were either in love with themselves, her money, or her body. Over the last couple of years, she'd had more than her fair share of proposals, but only one she'd even considered. She'd dated her father's young protégé, Mark DeVries, on and off for a year. He seemed like a nice enough guy, but she just didn't love him. Recently though, he'd been making bold attempts to seduce her, and her feelings of friendship had quickly turned to intense dislike for him and his insulting attempts.

She honestly didn't care about the inheritance money for herself, but her father needed it desperately and soon. The only way to save her father's trucking business was to get married. But could she marry someone she didn't love? That was the question she kept asking herself.

Standing six feet tall, legs apart and hands in pockets, John Northland stared out his second-floor office window toward the immense parking lot below. Semi-trucks, new and used, were lined up in neat rows. The smell of diesel exhaust fumes rose up through the small, open office window. Trucking was his life. Northland Trucking was in the business of selling and servicing semi-trucks and had been for thirty long years. Acquiring just two trucks to sell, he started the business and watched it grow to sales of over two hundred trucks a year.

Recently, due to a falling economy, sales hadn't been good. With the high fuel prices, high federal and state road usage taxes, and a dwindling economy, the independent truckers were hurting along with the fleets. And when truckers were hurting, they kept their old trucks and repaired them instead of buying new trucks.

John got caught holding the bag, you'd say. He ended up with a large truck inventory, most of which was on short-term loans at the bank. At this point, he could barely give the trucks away for cost. Finally, he'd been forced to take out a two-year personal note for two million dollars, due on July 31st of this year. The economy had finally started moving again, his business dramatically improved and was holding its own, but wasn't making enough to pay back the bank loan. As a last resort, today he'd met the bank president over lunch to see about an extension on the loan. The answer was no. The bank did not feel John would be able to repay the loan with the current economic situation, even down the line. The best thing to do would be to liquidate the business to obtain the money.

Pacing the floor of his office, searching for an answer, John knew his only hope was Brittany, his daughter. Running his thin fingers through his slightly receding gray hair, he headed for the soft leather chair behind his massive wood desk, tired of the pacing already. "Damn!" he shouted. "If only she'd gotten married!" His voice gradually became a whisper upon realizing his efficient secretary would hear. Sure enough, within minutes the door opened to his office.

"Everything all right?" asked Penny in a soft voice.

"Yes! Yes. I'm fine. Now don't disturb me again. I'll call you if I need anything," he answered in an irritated voice.

"Sorry," she apologized as she closed the door.

Slowly tapping his restless fingers on the empty desktop, his thoughts raced back to Brittany. Why did she have to be looking for a knight in shining armor? God only knows she had plenty of good prospects to choose from. And he knew, because he'd chosen most of them, without her knowledge of course, but none had been good enough for his Brittany. To collect her two-million-dollar inheritance from her grandfather, she had to marry by Saturday. Her grandfather had been old when he wrote the will, and he had old-fashioned ideas. In the will he stipulated she be married by her twenty-fifth birthday, June 30, to inherit the money, or wait till her thirtieth birthday. He must've assumed women didn't know how to handle money. That was the only reason he could think of to explain it.

Brittany was never interested in the money until the last few years when his company started to go downhill. She knew the loan was due soon, but she hoped the company would make enough to pay it off. So she'd waited and hoped.

If only she'd agree to marry Mark, his young assistant. Mark was a nice enough guy, but Brittany had made it very plain a friendship was all she wanted where Mark was concerned. And the poor guy had tried just about everything possible to convince her to marry him.

Hell! What was he to do with only one week left? If only Brittany would listen to him. It had actually gotten to the point he really didn't care who Brittany married, as long as she married by Saturday.

The damn phone rang, disturbing his thoughts. Pushing the button down, he stormed, "Now what do you want? I told you not to disturb me."

"Sorry, John, but I thought you'd want to know," she answered in a demure voice.

"Know what, Penny?" John asked impatiently.

"It's Mark. He found out Brittany left for the mountains this morning, and he's going out there after her. I just thought you'd like to know," she stated.

"There's not much I can do if he wants to try to change her mind. Although I don't think he stands a chance of succeeding, I do wish him the best of luck. Thanks for letting me know, Penny." John leaned back in his chair as he flipped the phone button off with a slight feeling of hope once again.

Mark DeVries was in a rage even though his face showed no trace of emotion. Early that morning, passing through the shop's service area, he overheard some mechanics talking about the Golden Girl. The truck was made road-ready late last night, so Brittany could leave at dawn. Damn! She'd slipped out on him again. Well, she couldn't go far enough to get rid of him.

Mark was the assistant general manager of Northland Trucking, working under her father, John. He was John's right-hand man, having worked his way up through the ranks of the business during the last four years.

Mark grew up poor, in a family where ample food and new clothing were considered luxuries. When he was ten years old, his father ran out on his mother and their family of four. He worked odd jobs ever since high school to help pay the bills and keep a roof over their heads. Mark was definitely his own man. He put himself through college on scholarships and worked a full-time job to support his family.

Thankfully, he was intelligent enough to earn straight A's without much effort or he never would've made it. Mark's childhood hadn't been easy, and as far as he was concerned, there was only one person to blame—his father. Not that it would've mattered one way or the other, since his father never could hold down a job anyway. His father was an alcoholic, so staying wouldn't have been of much help to any of them.

Mark, an embittered man of twenty-five, kept a calm composure not allowing it to show. He stood just under six feet tall with a firm, muscled body. His hair was thick and coal-black with natural curls descending over a high forehead. His face was distinctly carved including a somewhat large nose and a definite masculine jawline. His baby blue eyes flashed an authoritative sexy gleam that set many hearts aflutter.

Because of his effect on women, he managed to attract Brittany's attention for a while and began to put his plan into action. One way or another he was going to marry her, and the Northland Trucking business empire her father built would one day be his. Things had been going well with Brittany, until he'd started getting impatient and scared her off. He made big plans for dinner and the theater tonight, knowing she would be back home from her trip up north where she'd been hiding. Who would've thought she'd take off right away! She was most likely on her way to the mountains by now. If he left now, drove straight through, and didn't encounter any highway patrols, the mountains would be in view by nine or ten p.m.

Mark's plan was to obtain the Northland Trucking Company, the money and prestige it would bring, and Brittany would be the cream to top it off. Yes, he would enjoy all aspects of their inevitable union. If he played his cards right, he just might be sharing her bed soon. He'd waited long enough. She would be his, and with a little luck it would be legal, too. Mark had a bright outlook on their meeting. Knowing her kind heart, she would marry to save her father from financial ruin, and as far as he knew, he was the only person she would even consider marrying.